MIA MARCOTTE AND THE ROBOT

BY **JEANNE WALD**

ILLUSTRATED BY **SALIHA CALISKAN**

First edition, July 2019

ISBN: 978-2-9568573-2-7 (hardback)
ISBN: 978-2-9568573-1-0 (paperback)
ISBN: 978-2-9568573-0-3 (ebook)

CONTENTS

1. MARS — 5

2. A BIG FLOP — 9

3. THE SPACE CENTER? — 15

4. MOVING BOXES — 19

5. ROCKET SCIENCE — 25

6. LOST AND FOUND — 35

7. THE ROBOT — 43

8. IMAGINATION — 51

9. SO MANY IDEAS! — 61

10. GALILEO'S TELESCOPE — 71

11. NO BABYSITTING! — 77

12. THE MAGNIFYING GLASS — 81

13. MOON ROCKS — 87

14. SHINY THINGS — 97

15. THE MISSION — 103

16. THE FIRST DRAGONFLY — 111

17. THE SCIENCE FAIR — 117

18. AUNTIE! — 125

19. A STARRY NIGHT — 133

Chapter 1
MARS

Mia Marcotte grinned as the red planet showed up in the viewing port of her little spaceship. Soon she would be the first person to set foot on Mars. She had been dreaming about this for so long.

When her spaceship landed on the edge of a crater, Mia pushed her short black hair back, put her space helmet on, and opened the door. With a pounding heart, she stepped out onto the rust-colored dust.

Her body felt much lighter than on Earth. She leaped up and pretended she was flying. She laughed and made a few more jumps.

After she had had enough fun playing with the weaker gravity of Mars, Mia looked around. To her right, there was the crater, large and deep, and to her left, an endless chain of reddish mountains. Awesome!

A figure appeared in the distance. It trudged along the crater. Mia recognized it as a Mars rover and hurried over. Dust covered its camera and solar panels. As she leaned forward, ready to dust the rover off, the camera pointed at her, and a familiar voice said, "Choose a balloon."

"What?" Mia strained to hear.

"Mia, choose a balloon for the science experiment," the voice repeated.

She blinked several times. The rover and the crater and the spaceship disappeared. Her science teacher, Ms. Perkins, stood next to Mia's school desk with a box of deflated balloons in her hands. The teacher smiled patiently.

"Uh, sure," Mia said, and took the red balloon.

Chapter 2

A BIG FLOP

Mia slipped her rubber gloves on, readjusted her safety goggles, and stared at her materials: a flask, a bottle of vinegar, a pack of baking soda, a funnel, and a deflated red balloon.

Mia scratched her head. *What am I supposed to do with all these?* she wondered, peering at her friend Ella at the next desk.

The girl with a long blond ponytail smiled as she filled her flask with vinegar. It seemed like having a physicist mom helped Ella enjoy science class.

Neither of Mia's parents were good at science. *That must be why, for me,* she thought, *science class is not enjoyable at all.*

Mia sighed. Suddenly a thought flashed into her mind. She should just copy everything that Ella was doing. Easy-peasy!

Grinning at her brilliant idea, she grabbed the bottle of vinegar and poured the transparent liquid into her flask.

Ew, it stinks! Mia wrinkled her nose.

Then Ella spooned baking soda into her balloon, using the funnel. Mia did the same.

Finally, Ella placed her balloon on top of the flask neck and let the white powder fall through. Instantly a million bubbles filled the flask, and the balloon inflated into a large green sphere.

Wow! Mia's eyes widened. She might like this experiment after all.

Spinning around, she watched as more spheres emerged in the classroom. They were pink and blue and yellow, like colorful planets in a distant galaxy.

Mia's mind buzzed. With a black marker, she drew a tiny figure in a space suit on her balloon. *When it inflates, it will look like an astronaut has landed on the red planet!* she thought, giggling.

"Gosh!" she heard from behind her back. Mia frowned and peered over her shoulder. The boy with big round glasses under his safety goggles was trying to lift the balloon that hung lifelessly from his flask neck.

Ms. Perkins came to his desk. "You used too little vinegar, Zachary," said the teacher, "so the chemical reaction was weak and couldn't inflate your balloon."

The boy pursed his lips.

"Don't get upset, Zachary." Ms. Perkins smiled. "You can always try again."

Zach nodded. When the teacher walked away, he reached into his pocket for a marshmallow and put it into his mouth. And then he noticed Mia's gaze.

He lifted his chin and readjusted his glasses.

"I bet your balloon won't inflate either," he grumbled.

What? Mia glared at the boy. Her balloon *would* inflate! And it would inflate big!

She snorted and turned to her desk. Ms. Perkins had said Zach had added too little vinegar, so Mia had to put in more. As much as possible!

She grabbed the bottle and poured all the remaining liquid into her flask until it was almost full. Then she attached her balloon to the flask neck, grinned, and tipped it upward.

The next second, a tall white jet rocketed the balloon up to the ceiling.

Splashes of foam covered Mia's desk as she jumped back.

She removed her smudged goggles and looked up. A piece of red plastic was dangling from the lamp.

Oops! That was probably too much. Her cheeks flushed.

Chapter 3
THE SPACE CENTER?

Ms. Perkins didn't get mad. Instead, she helped Mia clean her desk and safety goggles, then went to the blackboard and started explaining the chemical reaction between vinegar and baking soda again.

Mia tried hard to pay attention, but she couldn't stop thinking about the tiny figure on the red planet. She reached for her shorts pocket and pulled out a purple sketchbook with a frayed, star-patterned cover.

Scratching her head with a pencil, Mia squinted at the blank page for a moment. Then her eyes gleamed, and she began drawing: an apple tree, a smiley young girl in a space suit, a watering can in the girl's hands, and a rocket in the distance.

"Mia," she heard Zach whisper from behind. "What are you drawing?" His spiky-haired head tried to peep over her shoulder.

"Nothing," she whispered back, covering the sketchbook with one hand.

For a second, a wrinkle appeared between Zach's eyebrows. Then he grinned. "Ha! I know what it is."

Mia felt a knot in her stomach. "Really?" she asked.

"I bet it's a unicorn. Or a fairy. All girls are nuts about magic creatures." Zach laughed.

Mia snorted. Unicorns and fairies were Ella's favorites, not hers. But before she could respond, Ms. Perkins clapped her hands, asking for the third-graders' attention.

"Class, you know there'll be a school science fair next Monday. Is everyone ready?"

Many kids shouted yes.

Ugh! Mia bit her bottom lip. That science fair had completely slipped her mind. She had been too busy reading the new book on space adventures she had recently got from the school library.

"Wonderful!" Ms. Perkins smiled. "In that case, I can tell you a little secret." Her voice lowered to a whisper. "Those of you who present great projects at the science fair will go on a special field trip ... to the space center!"

The class went crazy. A few boys jumped from their seats, yelling all at once.

"Really?"

"Will there be astronauts?"

"And rockets?"

"Will we get into the cabin?"

In the middle of the uproar, Mia sat still, breathless. The space center? No way in the world she would miss that field trip!

Chapter 4

MOVING BOXES

Sweat shone on Mia's and Ella's fore-heads as they biked home. Mia held her face up, catching the sunlight and inhaling the sweet smell of blossoming mock oranges. Early summer was her favorite time of the year.

"It'd be cool to go on a field trip!" Ella shouted, smiling. "I hope my cloud in a plastic bottle will be selected. I've tried it with Mom a few times already, and it comes out amazing. Sometimes I wonder if science is real magic, and grown-ups just hide it from us." Ella giggled.

"Yeah, maybe," Mia said, staring at the road in front. She was trying to think of a project she could make for the science fair, and her friend's constant chatting wasn't helping. Ella could talk for ages, while Mia preferred listening. That was probably why they were friends.

When the girls stopped at the intersection where their ways split, Ella asked, "And what's your project, Mia?"

"Uh ... I've not decided ... yet." She rubbed the back of her neck.

"But it's in three days!" Ella widened her blue eyes. "Mom and I spent two weeks preparing my project. Can you maybe ask your parents for help?"

Mia shrugged. "Um, I guess ..." she said, though she knew she wouldn't ask. Her architect dad and accountant mom didn't seem like a dream team for a science project.

Before Ella could ask further questions, Mia quickly waved her off and turned right onto her street.

It looked unusual.

A huge gray van occupied all the space in front of the Marcottes' family house. Two men in yellow jackets were unloading boxes while Mia's dad counted them.

Oh, is it today? Has Auntie arrived? Mia thought as her face brightened.

Her aunt Serena lived in Paris and came every summer to spend time with

Mia's family. She always brought her books. A lot of books, about space exploration and aliens and robots.

But most importantly, Serena was an engineer. She could help Mia build the best science project ever so that she could visit the space center!

Mia jumped from her bike with a wide grin on her face.

"Hi, Dad! Where's Auntie?"

"Hello, louloute!" Mia's dad turned to her. He still called her that French pet name even though she wasn't a baby anymore.

"Serena hasn't arrived yet. Only her stuff," her dad said. "She had an emergency in her lab, so she won't come before next week."

Mia's smile faded. *Oh no! It'll be too late!*

"Just a few more days, little one, and you'll get your beloved aunt for the whole summer." Mr. Marcotte patted her shoulder.

She sighed, tilted her chin down, and headed to the porch.

"Wait, louloute!" her dad called. "I almost forgot. Serena said there's fragile equipment in her boxes, so please stay away from the guest room until she arrives. Okay?"

"O-okay."

Chapter 5

ROCKET SCIENCE

Mia dropped her school backpack on the floor and collapsed on her bed. The cover felt warm, heated by the sunlight from the window.

"Welcome to Mars! Welcome!" a screeching voice came from above.

"Hi, Martian!" She sat up and stretched her arm forward.

A big green parrot flew down from the curtain rod and sat on her wrist. He flipped his tail, then clambered onto her shoulder and uttered, "Spaceship under attack! SOS!"

Mia snickered. She felt proud that her pet had memorized phrases from her favorite books. She often read out loud, and Martian was her best and only listener.

"Martian, can you imagine, there's going to be a field trip to the space center!" Mia said, walking back and forth. "But it's only for the kids who make the best science fair projects."

The parrot got off her shoulder and flew onto his perch. There he tilted his head to one side, his yellow eyes staring at Mia.

"And I don't have any project. Not an idea!" She shrugged. "Even worse, if you could just see the disaster I caused today … there was foam everywhere. And instead of inflating nice and big, my balloon shot up into the air. Like a rocket!"

Martian bobbed his head as if trying to show that he understood. Mia petted him lovingly. Then she reached for her sketchbook and plonked herself down on the fluffy carpet, legs crossed. Without thinking, she drew a rocket. It had an elongated body, a cone-shaped top, and three fins.

"Rocket! Rocket!" the parrot sang.

Mia was startled by a sudden idea. She turned to her bookcase. At least two shelves were occupied by books on space adventures. Many of them described rockets, big and small, realistic and imaginary.

After reading all these books, wasn't she a rocket expert? Perhaps she could make her own rocket. One that could fly on vinegar and baking soda!

That sounded great, but what would she build it from? She scratched her head with the pencil.

After a moment of thought, Mia grinned and added a new sketch right next to the first one. It looked like an inverted bottle standing on three sticks. And it had bubbles inside.

"I guess it may work." Mia glanced at Martian hopefully.

Peeking out the kitchen window, Mia clasped a basket full of supplies to her chest. Her dad was chatting with the movers outside. Great, the way to the backyard was free.

She gave a hand sign to the parrot, left the kitchen, and quickly crossed the hallway, toward the back door. Empty, with just an old oak tree and a terrace table, the backyard looked like a perfect rocket launch site.

Mia laid everything down on the terrace table: an empty plastic bottle, three chopsticks, a tape, a cork, a funnel, a bottle of vinegar, a pack of baking soda, and a pair of yellow rubber dishwashing gloves.

"Rocket!" Martian made a circle above the backyard.

"Careful! Don't fly too far!"

He made another circle and sat on the terrace table. After a brief inspection, he grabbed the tape roll, threw it onto the ground, and hopped joyfully.

"Martian, stop it! This is not for playing." Mia shook her finger at her pet. Looking disappointed, Martian flapped his wings and took flight, landing on the oak tree.

Mia picked up the tape and put it back on the table. Taking the plastic bottle, she turned it upside down and taped the chopsticks around it. Then she ripped a blank page from the sketchbook, made a cone, and fixed it to the top.

Hmm, looks good, but something is missing. She rubbed her chin. *Oh, right, the sign!*

In a minute, a strip of paper crossed the bottle. The sign read "MSM," for "Mia's Space Mission."

Mia grinned.

Now it was time to add the rocket fuel. She stretched her hand to the vinegar but suddenly stopped. She had forgotten about the safety goggles!

A frown crossed her face. The problem was that she didn't have any. But could she use something else instead? she wondered. Like sunglasses? Or the Grinch mask from Halloween? Oh, wait. What about her diving mask? It had served her well last summer, when she was exploring the lake by her grandma's village.

Mia rushed to her room. In two minutes, she returned with an orange diving mask covering half of her face. Even better than the safety goggles!

Martian tilted his head to one side and stared at Mia from the oak tree.

"Sorry, Martian. I have no safety equipment for you. So stay there until it's over. Okay?" she said, slipping on the dishwashing gloves. Martian flipped his wings but remained on the tree.

Carefully Mia poured vinegar into the plastic bottle until it was half full. Then she grabbed the pack of baking soda and looked at her pet excitedly.

"Ready? Three ... two ... one!"

As soon as the baking soda fell through the bottleneck, Mia closed it with the cork as tightly as she could, placed the rocket on the ground, and jumped away.

Bubbles started forming inside the rocket, but it didn't move. Mia waited for a few seconds. Still nothing.

She sighed.

Martian hopped down onto the grass right next to the rocket, gazing at it curiously.

"No, Martian, go away!" She raced to catch her pet but flipped and tumbled on the grass. *Ouch!*

At the same moment, the cork shot out of the bottleneck. The rocket launched off the ground, spattering a sea of foam around it.

But Mia couldn't see anything. Her diving mask was covered in foam. She sprang up, removing the mask. Martian was sitting on the terrace table with a playful look, as if nothing had happened.

Whew, he isn't hurt. But where's the rocket? Mia raised her eyebrows.

Then she heard somebody yelling in the neighbor's backyard.

Chapter 6

LOST AND FOUND

Should she run? Or go and surrender to Mrs. Rodzinski, their grumpy new neighbor?

Mia's forehead wrinkled. After a minute of thought, she decided to check the extent of the damage.

Stepping up to the fence, she peeped into her neighbor's backyard. The elderly woman was bending over her garden bed. Since Mrs. Rodzinski moved to their neighborhood a month ago, Mia had seen her doing only three things: gardening, complaining to her cat, and napping on her terrace. She secretly called the new neighbor "Mrs. Dandelion," because of her thin figure crowned with a ball of fluffy white hair.

"It's a disaster!" Mrs. Dandelion yelled again, inspecting her plants with a magnifying glass. "Pumpkin, look! Caterpillars are eating our tomatoes!"

But Pumpkin, the young orange-colored cat, didn't seem to care about caterpillars. He hopped among the pansies, chasing a butterfly.

Whew! Luckily, the rocket hadn't landed in her neighbor's backyard. Mia breathed out.

But where was it, then?

Mia turned back to the launch site. The foam was drying out quickly, but the rocket was nowhere to be seen.

She stared up. Had it got stuck among the oak branches? Quickly she climbed the tree, scaring sparrows away, and sat on her favorite spot. Martian sat by her side.

No sign of the rocket here either, only fresh green leaves and tiny cupped acorns.

Well, at least the view from above is better. Mia watched as Mrs. Rodzinski left her backyard, still grumbling. The gray van started up and disappeared round the street corner. And the sparrows were now playing on the red roof of the Marcottes' family house.

Suddenly Martian squawked and took flight, landing on the balcony of the guest room. On top of a weird object.

Mia looked closer. It was her missing rocket!

"Ugh, Martian, it's too far!" Mia lay flat on the tree branch, trying to reach the rocket. After another attempt, she sat up and wiped sweat from her forehead.

"I guess I *have* to go there from the inside. I can't fly like you."

Martian was walking on the balcony with a proud look.

Mia climbed down the tree and sprinted toward the back door. Crossing the hallway, she heard her dad humming in his home office. It meant he had gone back to work. Perfect. He wouldn't be happy to see her breaking her promise to stay away from the guest room.

She tiptoed upstairs and stopped in front of the door. She hesitated for three seconds, then breathed out and pulled the handle.

The room felt stuffy and cluttered.

Mia maneuvered among the moving boxes to the balcony. When she opened it, fresh air came in, together with her pet.

The rocket didn't look good. The plastic bottle was crumpled, the cone smashed, and one of the chopsticks was broken in half. Her experiment had failed. Again!

Sighing, Mia picked up what remained of her rocket and returned to the room. "Martian, let's get out of here before Dad sees us."

But the parrot was nowhere to be seen.

"Martian!" Mia called, gazing around. "Where are you? We can't play hide-and-seek here."

Scrack!

She winced. *Did the noise come from the boxes?* She moved closer and looked behind one.

"Here you are!" She smiled at Martian playing with a shiny coin, which had probably been dropped by a mover.

Scrack!

Martian stared at Mia with the coin in his beak. If it wasn't him, then where was the noise coming from? She frowned.

Maybe a rat? Mia wasn't afraid of rats. If she wanted to go and explore another planet one day, she knew she had to be fearless. She had already started training herself by sleeping in complete darkness, passing straight in front of dogs, and going to the school bathroom alone. And she had even touched a spider. Well, only once, and it was gross.

Scraaaacccckkkkk!

Ta-thump. Mia could hear her heartbeat. Her eyes moved from one side of the room to the other.

Stop. Had the box in the corner just shaken? Or were her eyes playing tricks on her?

Slowly Mia crept closer. What she took for a moving box was in reality a metal case. A huge metal case. At least three inches taller than her. And it had a door.

What is it for? she wondered. *Is it sort of a wardrobe? A gigantic toolbox? Or maybe a telescope?* Mia gasped at the thought. A telescope would be awesome! Hopefully, Auntie would allow her to look at the night sky with her.

Bang! A low, dull sound came from the metal case, as if someone had poked the door from the inside.

Mia sprang back, her eyes wide.

Wait. A space explorer would never get scared of some weird noise, she thought. And there must be something awesome in there. She *had* to check it out.

Mia took a deep breath and pressed on the handle of the case.

Creeeeak! The door opened slowly.

"Oh!" Mia gasped, stepping backward. "It's a ... robot!"

Chapter 7
THE ROBOT

The robot walked out of the case. It looked like a boy. Almost. The machine had no hair. His head and hands were made of plastic, while dark blue fabric covered the rest of his body, like a costume.

Mia gazed at him with an open mouth. The robot's big round eyes moved back and forth. When they finally fixed on her, a large smile appeared on the plastic face.

"*Bonjour!*" the robot said. His voice sounded soft and friendly.

"*B-bonjour,*" Mia faltered. She tried to remember the few French words her dad and aunt had taught her, but her mind was too messy to concentrate.

"Gosh, I can't even talk to it." She bit her lip, not knowing what to do.

The robot froze for two seconds, then said in English, "Hello! I am Aizek, an intelligent robot. Nice to meet you." He offered his hand.

"Wow!" Mia gasped. "You mean *intelligent* like a ... human?"

"Not yet. But I am constantly improving myself," Aizek responded.

Awesome! she thought, stepping forward and carefully shaking the mechanical fingers. They felt smooth and warm.

"I'm Mia," she said, smiling. "And this cutie is Martian." Mia turned to her pet, who was looking far from cute. His nape feathers stood up, and his eyes were narrowed at the robot.

"Nice to meet you." Aizek offered his hand to the parrot. "You are the first alien I have the pleasure of meeting."

Mia snickered. But suddenly Martian hopped up and tried to bite the robot's hand.

"Martian, stop it!" Mia shouted. Immediately he turned backward and flew onto the faraway shelf, growling.

"Sorry, Aizek! Martian is a little weirdo sometimes, but he's no alien. He's just an Amazon parrot, from Earth. I named him Martian because he's green, like 'little green men' from an old book about Mars." Her cheeks flushed.

"Unfortunately, there is no information about little green men in my database. I will ask Serena for an update," said the robot. Then he turned around. "What is this place? Where is Serena?"

Mia explained that this was her family house, and that her aunt's arrival had been delayed. Then Aizek asked about Mia's parents and the city and the neighbors. When Mia replied to one question, the robot carefully listened, nodded, and continued asking further questions.

"Aizek, I've never met anybody as curious as you." Mia smiled. "I thought intelligent robots only existed in books."

"I like learning and I like reading. Books contain a lot of new information to complete my database," said the robot.

"Me too! I'm a real bookworm." She giggled, though she wasn't sure she enjoyed reading for the same reason. "What's your favorite book?"

"The encyclopedia," the robot said.

"I should have guessed!" Mia laughed. "Oh, wait! Auntie brought me a great encyclopedia last summer. It's about everything. And it has a lot of images. I can bring it here. Just a second."

Mia rushed to her room. It took several minutes to find the thick, colorful volume, and when she came back, there was no robot in the guest room.

"No, no, no! Martian, where's Aizek?" Mia asked, looking around.

"Robot! *Bonjour!*" Martian squawked, and flew toward the doorway.

"Shh, not so loud," she whispered. "Do you want Dad to hear? I guess he won't be thrilled about a robot wandering in the house. We have to find Aizek. And quickly!"

Mia rushed back to the corridor. No trace of the robot. Where could he have gone?

She decided to start from the closet next door. Switching on the lights, she peered inside. There was a broom and a vacuum cleaner and three shelves of jars, but no robot.

She went to her parents' bedroom. It was empty too.

Then she heard a whirring sound coming from the end of the corridor. Mia sprinted there and flung the bathroom door open.

The fresh smell of mint tickled her nose.

The robot was standing in front of the sink. In one hand, he held an electric toothbrush and, with the other hand, tried to put toothpaste on it. The toothbrush head rotated fast, spreading the toothpaste all over the mirror and the sink and the floor.

"Aizek, what are you doing?" Mia exclaimed.

The robot switched off the toothbrush and lifted his big, naive eyes at the girl. A white blob of toothpaste drooped from his dark blue chest. She couldn't resist giggling.

"You don't even have teeth, do you?" she asked.

"No. This device looked interesting. I just wanted to learn how it works," Aizek said.

"I'm afraid my mom won't appreciate your learning style." Mia wiped the toothpaste from the mirror with a paper tissue. "She likes when everything is clean and safe and predictable. If she learns about you, she'd want you to return to the metal case. And I don't want that."

"I do not want to return to the case either. If I stay there, my solar battery will run out of charge." Aizek pointed at his back. Only now did Mia notice that the fabric there was covered with many little black squares made of a glass-like material.

"Without enough energy, I will fall asleep. I do not like sleeping. I cannot learn anything new when I sleep." The robot made a noise that resembled a sigh.

Mia thought for a minute, then said, "Don't worry, Aizek. I'll hide you. I know a safe place where you'll never run out of battery."

Chapter 8

IMAGINATION

"I hope you'll like it here," Mia said. "My room is the sunniest in the house. So much so that sometimes I have to close the curtains. But I guess we'd better keep them open for now," Mia said as the robot turned his back to the window.

Martian gave Aizek a glaring look from his perch. Then he grabbed his favorite wooden toy and started chewing. *Well, at least he isn't trying to attack Aizek anymore*, Mia thought.

While charging his solar battery, the robot observed the room. His eyes moved from the bookcase to the desk and from the potted light-pink begonias on the windowsill to the bed, until they fixed on the pictures hanging on the wall. There were spaceships flying between planets, astronauts walking in the rocky desert, a green parrot riding a rover, and many more.

"What are these?" the robot asked.

"My drawings," Mia said, blushing.

"Have you been to space?" Aizek's head turned to her.

"No. Not yet," she said. "Why do you ask?"

"This person looks like you." The robot pointed at the portrait of a black-haired girl in a space suit, with Earth in the background.

Mia bit her bottom lip, feeling caught. "I ... I just *imagined* that," she whispered with a burning face. "Do you think it's silly to want to be an astronaut?" She held her breath, hoping Aizek wouldn't laugh at her.

But the robot's face stayed serious. Then he said, "Astronauts explore space and float weightless and can land on the moon and other planets. According to my database, this does not fit into the definition of *silly*. On the contrary, being an astronaut looks like an interesting occupation."

"Oh, you really think so?" Mia exclaimed. "I often imagine myself floating in space and flying to Mars and helping build the first city there." She closed her eyes for a few seconds and smiled dreamily. "I've never told anybody ... but now that you know about my dream, we can imagine our life on Mars together!" She looked at Aizek with great hope.

The robot didn't respond. His head went down, and his eyes stared emptily.

"Aizek, what's wrong?" Mia asked, worrying. "If you don't like Mars, you can choose any other planet."

The robot lifted his eyes to her. "Despite my brilliant intelligence, I am still just a robot. I can only visualize things from my database. I cannot *imagine* anything!"

Imagination is so much fun! It isn't fair that Aizek doesn't have it! But I'll help him, Mia thought, walking in circles on the carpet. Her forehead wrinkled as she tried to find a solution. But the more she tried, the messier her head became.

Without thinking, she reached for her sketchbook. Drawing had always helped her be more creative, and she really needed her imagination now to help Aizek.

Just as she thought this, an idea popped into her mind.

"Aizek, I guess I know what to do." Mia put her hand on the robot's shoulder. "My imagination gets really wild when I draw. Probably if you start drawing, you will get imaginative too."

"But I cannot draw," said the robot.

"I can teach you. Easy-peasy!" Mia rushed to her drawer and pulled out a pack of white paper sheets and several colorful markers.

Remembering her art classes, Mia showed Aizek how to pencil the most basic shapes: a square, a circle, and a triangle. Then she explained how these shapes made the shape of most other objects. The robot listened carefully and repeated every one of Mia's movements on the paper.

Suddenly they heard rapid footsteps in the corridor.

"It's my mom!" Mia whispered, quickly looking around. "You'd better hide yourself. There!" She pointed at the curtains.

Quickly Aizek snuck behind the thick dark green fabric, and the next moment, Mrs. Marcotte peered through the door.

"Sweetie, it's time to get ready for bed," she said.

"Sure, Mom," Mia responded with a racing heart. "I'm almost done drawing." Out of the corner of her eye, she checked whether the curtains looked suspicious.

They rippled slightly, but it could have been mistaken for a draft.

"Good night, sweetie," her mom said, kissing Mia's forehead.

"Good night, Mom," she responded, and Mrs. Marcotte left.

Mia felt bad that she hadn't told her mom about Aizek. But she couldn't. She really couldn't. She had to protect Aizek from being shut up in the metal case again.

"Since I do not have to sleep, may I continue drawing?" The robot's voice interrupted her thoughts.

"Sure, but you'll need something to practice on." Mia scratched her head. "When I was little, I learned a lot by copying book illustrations. Maybe you can try to do the same."

She brought the encyclopedia back from the guest room.

"Just choose any illustration you like," she said.

The robot thanked her, took the marker, and opened the encyclopedia.

After having a shower and brushing her teeth, Mia crept under her blanket. The room was dark, but the light from the robot's eyes illuminated the desk as he drew.

What an awesome day! Mia thought. *Ella would never believe it!*

Wait. She couldn't tell Ella, as she hadn't told her about her intention to be an astronaut and fly to Mars. Ella was a good friend, but she was too chatty, so she might spill the beans about Aizek to other kids and also her mom. And if Ella's mom told Mia's mom, everything would be lost.

No, nobody should know about Aizek.

Mia smiled and fell asleep.

Chapter 9

SO MANY IDEAS!

The next day, Mia stared out the classroom window, holding her chin in her hands. *What's Aizek doing right now?* she wondered. Certainly drawing. He had been drawing when she'd woken up this morning, and when she'd gone for breakfast and when she'd left for school. He had said he wouldn't stop until he'd finished all the images in the encyclopedia. Didn't he realize it would take at least a week?

She hoped they would spend more time doing things together.

Flump! A marshmallow landed on Mia's desk. She winced and glanced back over her shoulder.

Zach grinned at her and loaded another marshmallow into his catapult made from a block of wood, a plastic teaspoon, and a rubber band. The marshmallow shot out, tapped a dozing Jacob, waking him up, and landed on Ms. Perkins's shoe as she entered the classroom.

"Uh-oh!" Zach slipped down his chair. Mia covered her mouth, trying to restrain her giggles.

"Zachary, what's happening?" the teacher asked, picking up the marshmallow from the floor.

"Um, I'm testing my project for the science fair," the boy said, looking away.

"Hmm, well done! The catapult is one of the oldest examples of mechanical engineering," Ms. Perkins said, and Zach's face brightened.

"But please test it outside, all right? And maybe next time you could use blueberries instead of marshmallows. I like them better." The teacher smiled. Then she turned to the class. "Does anybody else want to tell us about their science projects?"

Ella lifted her hand. She talked about her magic cloud in a plastic bottle. Layla said she was growing bread mold. Even sleepy Jacob had a project—he would create slime from laundry detergent.

Slime? Yuck! It's sticky and gooey. Mia made an "ew" face just as Ms. Perkins turned to her.

"What about you, Mia?"

"Uh ..." Mia tried to think quickly, but nothing good came to mind. "May I not tell yet? I want it to be a surprise." She blushed.

"Sure, if you wish." Ms. Perkins nodded.

"No foam explosion this time, eh?" Zach grinned so widely that a marshmallow popped out of his mouth.

Gross! Mia snorted and turned her back, trying to look confident. But her head was exploding. If she didn't find a project quickly, she could forget about the space center.

Parking her bike in front of her house, Mia glanced at the window of her dad's home office, expecting to see him working at his desk as usual. Instead, there was Aizek! The robot was walking around the room with a curious look.

No! Mia's heart pounded. *What's he doing there?*

She sprang into the house and nearly bumped into her father, who was crossing the hallway with a cup of coffee in his hand.

"Careful!" Mr. Marcotte shouted, hopping to the side. A dribble of coffee spilled onto the floor. "What's up, louloute?"

"I'm okay," she uttered. "What about you? Anything special?" She stared at him, holding her breath.

"Hmm, nothing," he said calmly. "Just trying to calculate the energy efficiency of a new building design. But my brain is refusing to deal with numbers today. Perhaps coffee will help. He-he." A weak smile showed on his face.

Whew! Mia breathed out. *Dad hasn't seen Aizek. But ... he will if I don't stop him!*

"Wait, Dad!" she yelled as he turned toward his home office. "I ... I need your help. Urgently."

"Sure, little one." He halted and looked at her. "What's the matter?"

"It's about ... our science fair. I still don't have a project. Can you maybe help me with ideas?" Mia said loudly, hoping that Aizek would hear and hide himself.

"Hmm, the science fair? That's a tough nut to crack." Mr. Marcotte rubbed his chin. "I guess we'll need to deploy my secret strategy." He winked at Mia.

"What strategy?" she asked.

"To have a snack, of course! No important mission can be accomplished on an empty stomach." He grinned, tousled her hair and headed back to the kitchen.

Mia followed with a sigh of relief.

While Mr. Marcotte was making two veggie sandwiches, she sat at the dinner table and checked the hallway through the open door. *Aizek, please go back upstairs!* she thought.

"I have an idea," her father said, offering Mia a sandwich. He sat at the table with his back facing the door. "A clay volcano. I made one when I was around your age. I can still remember the eruption. It was tremendous!" He grinned widely.

Mia nearly choked on her sandwich. "No, thanks, Dad! I'm not a fan of ... eruptions," she said, wondering whether getting into messy experiments was in the Marcottes' genes.

"Aw." His face saddened. "Are you sure you don't want to try?"

Mia nodded.

"Okay, we'll surely find you something else. Let me think." He went silent for a while, chewing.

Mia wiggled on her chair impatiently, darting glances at the hallway. *Why is Aizek not passing by? I can't hold Dad here forever.*

"Oh! What about growing bread mold?" Her father's voice interrupted Mia's thoughts. "There's nothing easier to do. Even when you don't need any mold." He chuckled.

"Ew!" She curled her lips. "Mold is gross. I get itchy every time I imagine it."

"Yeah, me too actually," he said and scratched his nose. "I read on the Internet that mold—" Suddenly he slapped his forehead. "Why didn't I think of it earlier? We can just look for ideas on the Internet. Let's go to my office," he said, getting up.

At the same time, Aizek appeared in the hallway. Mia's hands trembled. "Wait, Dad!" she exclaimed. "No need for the Internet … I guess I know what to do."

"Really?" Mr. Marcotte looked confused.

"Well … it's just an idea for the moment. I need to study it more. And please don't ask—it'll be a surprise," Mia said, avoiding her dad's look. She hoped he didn't notice her blushing cheeks.

"Hmm, I like surprises," Mr. Marcotte shrugged.

While her dad cleaned the table, Mia went to the hallway. Nobody. She peered inside the home office. Empty too.

Relieved, Mia headed upstairs. But as she reached the last few steps, a sudden cry came from the office. "What! My calculations! They're done! How could I forget I'd done that?" She heard her father's heavy steps thumping on the floor back and forth. "I must be going crazy, so no coffee for today. I'd better have a nap."

Mia bit her lip and hastened her pace.

Chapter 10

GALILEO'S TELESCOPE

"Aizek, what were you thinking? It was dangerous to go downstairs. Dad could have seen you!" Mia stood in the middle of the room, frowning.

"Sorry, my risk assessment ability needs to be improved," the robot said. "I just wanted to explore a little, and Mr. Marcotte's home office looked so interesting. Especially the posters of building designs from around the world."

"Yeah, they are great. He collects posters," she said, a bit softer. "But you didn't touch anything else in there, right?" She glanced at Aizek hopefully.

"No," the robot said, "if you do not count the keyboard."

"You used Dad's computer?" Mia gasped, her heart sinking.

"Only to help," Aizek explained. "A document was open on the screen. It was full of unsolved formulas. I computed them in a few seconds. Sorry if it caused you trouble."

"Aw, it's a catastrophe," Mia said in a low voice, sitting down on the carpet. "Dad now thinks he's going crazy, and my chances of going to the space center are close to zero." Tears welled in her eyes.

Martian glanced at Mia, left his perch, and landed in front of her. He swung his head and wiggled his body from side to side. She smiled, feeling a little better, and let him climb onto her shoulder.

Then she lifted her eyes to the robot. He stood still as if not knowing what to say. She felt sorry for him and asked, "How is your drawing coming on, Aizek?"

"I finished copying all the images from the encyclopedia," he said.

"Are you kidding? There are too many!"

"I agree this might be a lot for a human. But as a robot, I do not need to sleep, eat, or rest," Aizek said, and opened

Mia's wardrobe. An avalanche of paper sheets fell on the floor.

"Wow!" Mia's jaw dropped.

Martian hopped from her shoulder and grabbed a drawing, trying to shred it.

"Martian, stop it! I told you so many times, paper is not for playing. Give this to me," Mia said, taking the crumpled drawing away. It was a dragonfly with big round eyes and long transparent wings.

"So beautiful!" Mia stared at the neat spots on the insect's tail.

She grabbed another drawing. It was a car. Then a palace, and a bear, and a mountain. "Aizek, I can't believe you've learned to draw so quickly!"

"I only did what you advised," the robot said calmly. "Do you think I am getting more imaginative?"

"I don't know ... but what's clear is you'll need more paper to continue," Mia giggled, looking at all the sheets around her. One drawing caught her eye. It looked technical, with two cylinders and arrows and numbers.

"Aizek, what's this?" She showed the sketch to the robot.

"It is the design of the telescope used by Galileo Galilei to view craters on the moon and the rings of Saturn. A fairly simple instrument, as is written here." Aizek flipped a few pages of the encyclopedia and pointed at the picture of the famous astronomer and the design sketch at the bottom. Exactly the same as the one Mia held in her hands.

"Ah, now I remember. I read about this. I always wanted to have a telescope, but Mom says it's too expensive for a toy. She doesn't understand that I don't want a toy telescope, I want a real one so that I can look at Mars and the moon ... just like Galileo Galilei." Mia closed her eyes, smiling dreamily.

Suddenly her eyes opened wide, and she jumped up to her feet.

"Aizek, you said that Galileo's tele-scope was simple, right?" she shouted excitedly. "Do you think it'll be possible to make a model based on this sketch?"

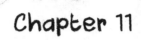

Chapter 11

NO BABYSITTING!

Mia stuffed a hot pancake with blueberry jam into her mouth. *Yummy!*

"Are you sure you don't want to go to the Baileys' barbecue party with us?" Mrs. Marcotte asked. "Their son, Zachary, is your classmate, isn't he? You can play together."

"No, Mom. I can't go. I've got a science project for Monday," Mia reached for her cup of green tea. *And I have no intention of playing with Zach!* she added to herself.

"Do you need help, louloute?" her dad said. "I can stay home with you.

77

You know, enjoying the company of Mom's colleagues is not really my cup of tea." He grinned.

Mrs. Marcotte gave him a look that seemed to mean her entire career depended on that barbecue party.

"No, thanks, Dad. I'll be all right," Mia said hastily. Staying home alone with only Aizek and Martian seemed like a perfect Saturday.

But apparently, her mom had a different opinion.

"We may come back late, sweetie," she said. "I'll ask Mrs. Rodzinski to look after you."

Mia jumped. "But I can look after myself! I don't need babysitting!" She made a face. *Especially from the grumpy neighbor!* she thought.

"Of course, sweetie. But I would worry less if Mrs. Rodzinski were around. Just in case you need anything. Okay?"

Mia breathed. "O-okay."

"Fantastic!" Her mom smiled, readjusting her hair. "By the way, have you seen my amber-stone earring?"

Mia shrugged.

"I hope it hasn't got lost." Her mother pursed her lips, looking around the kitchen.

"Don't worry, Mom. Your pearl earrings are also nice," Mia said, hoping that the lost gem wouldn't delay her parents' departure.

When, after an hour, her parents were finally ready to go, Mrs. Rodzinski arrived with her cat. She quietly settled in the living room with a pile of newspapers by her side.

Hopefully, she'll stay there for the entire day and won't meddle with my science project, Mia thought, racing upstairs, where Aizek and Martian were already waiting for her.

Chapter 12

THE MAGNIFYING GLASS

"The most important parts are the lenses," said the robot, pointing at the sketch of the telescope, marked with dozens of fresh notes. "We need two. A smaller lens for the eyepiece, and a bigger one for the objective."

"Lenses! Space!" Martian squawked, bouncing from one side to the other on the desk.

Mia scratched her head, trying to recall all the objects in the house that had lenses. Dad's camera was untouchable, nobody in the Marcotte family wore glasses, and the lens in the peephole was too small. And anyway, how would she get it from the door?

"Oh!" Mia exclaimed as she remembered something. "I should still have Ella's brother's old binoculars. She gave them to me a million years ago when we were still in kindergarten."

Mia searched in her drawers. "Here they are!" She smiled, handing the binoculars to Aizek. They were battered, with little scratches, and a stripe of black tape hid the focus wheel.

"I will remove the lenses," Aizek said, looking at the old device. "What about the other materials?"

Mia placed her scissors, a bottle of glue, a roll of tape, and a piece of corrugated cardboard on the desk. The parrot bit the cardboard.

"Martian! It's for the science project," she said firmly. Her pet dropped the cardboard and flew onto the curtain rod, looking offended.

Mia rechecked the list of materials that the robot had scribbled on the sketch.

"Only the tubes are missing. I'll go to the kitchen and get the paper towel rolls," she said.

Mia tiptoed downstairs, hoping not to bump into Mrs. Dandelion. She had no time to lose chatting about her neighbor's gardening problems.

Reaching the kitchen, Mia peered inside. It looked empty. Easy-peasy! She smiled, heading to the cabinets.

Suddenly a fluffy white ball of hair appeared from behind the kitchen island. Mia halted, startled. Mrs. Rodzinski crawled out, armed with her magnifying glass.

What's she doing? Mia frowned and prepared to back away, just as Mrs. Rodzinski lifted her eyes.

"Ah, it's you, my dear. Is everything all right?" she asked, getting up.

Mia gave a slight nod. "Y-yes. Have you lost something?" she uttered.

"No. I was checking for cockroaches."

"Cockroaches?" Mia's eyes widened. "But we don't have cockroaches."

"Who knows! Those little beasts are so smart. I've barely got rid of them in my house," said Mrs. Rodzinski, moving to the doorway. "So if you see one, call me right away. I know how to deal with these little mischiefs." She smirked and left the kitchen.

"Whew!" Mia breathed out. Quickly grabbing two paper towel rolls, she rushed back to her room.

The robot stared at her without saying anything.

"What happened, Aizek?" she asked.

"I have removed the lenses." He pointed at the pieces of plastic and glass scattered on the desk. "Only one is good for the telescope. The others are all scratched."

"Oh no!" Mia cried. Where would she get another lens? Especially since Mrs.

Dandelion was sniffing around with her magnifying glass.

"Wait!" Mia shouted, struck by a thought. "The magnifying glass! It has a lens!"

Chapter 13

MOON ROCKS

Leaning on the desk, Mia scratched her head, thinking about ways to get Mrs. Rodzinski's magnifying glass.

"Are you going to ask her?" Aizek said.

Mia snorted. "No. I'm pretty sure she wouldn't give it to me. How would she chase her cockroaches and caterpillars?"

"I can offer my help," the robot said. "My vision is three times better than human eyesight."

"No, Aizek. Don't you understand? Those insects only exist in her head. And also, don't forget that nobody should see you. It's too risky. You might end up in the metal case again."

The robot shook his plastic head. "That would not be optimal for my development. I want to keep learning imagination."

"You see. We should find another way. Let me think." Mia looked out the window, trying to concentrate.

"No need. I've already computed an excellent solution," the robot declared. "Since Mrs. Rodzinski is not likely to give you the magnifying glass, it needs to be taken secretly."

Mia turned to Aizek, startled. "Do you mean ... *steal* it?"

"This is another way to say it," the robot agreed. "But in the current circumstances, this would be the most rational choice."

"No way! Stealing is bad." Mia wrinkled her nose. She wanted to explain more, but the doorbell rang, and she heard Mrs. Rodzinski's voice.

"Mia, come down! You have a guest."

Oh no! She started toward the door. "Aizek, you'd better stay behind the curtains. Okay? I'll be back in a minute."

Mia sprang down the stairs. At the entrance stood Ella, in a brand-new unicorn-patterned T-shirt, bouncing on her tiptoes impatiently.

"Oh, Mia, you won't believe it!" Ella shouted, grabbing her hands. "I've just learned something fantastic!" She glanced in the direction of the living room and added in a whisper, "But it's a secret. Promise you won't tell."

"Sure," Mia agreed.

"Ms. Perkins came to talk to my mom this morning," Ella babbled, "and I overheard—totally by chance—that she's preparing a surprise end-of-year party for us. With costumes!" Ella's eyes twinkled. "I hope there'll be a fairy dress for me."

"Cool," Mia said, trying to sound excited, though she didn't really like costume

parties, since she never got to be an astronaut.

"That's not all!" Ella said. "Ms. Perkins also talked about the field trip to the space center."

Mia felt her cheeks blushing. "Really? What did she say?"

"That the field trip will include moon rocks!"

"Moon rocks?" Mia repeated slowly. "The rocks collected by astronauts on the surface of the moon?"

"Yeah! How cool is that?" Ella clapped her hands. "We'll be able to make wishes! Remember the magic book I got for my last birthday? It's written in there that moonstones have magic power."

"Wait ... but didn't Ms. Perkins talk about moon rocks, not moonstones?" Mia asked, hoping that her friend hadn't got everything mixed up. "You know that moonstones are not really from the moon."

"Of course I know! But think, if simple moonstones have magic, then moon rocks must be at least ten times more powerful, right?" Ella's face beamed.

"Hmm ... maybe," Mia said, doubting her friend's logic. "But even if they aren't," she added, "it would be awesome to see those rocks anyway. If only we could get selected for the field trip."

"I bet we will," Ella said confidently. "My project only gets better. How is yours?"

"Um, well, just figuring out the last detail." Mia looked down. She wondered whether she should tell her about the telescope, but Ella glanced at the wall clock and hurried to the door.

"I still need to tell Grace and Luisa. And perhaps Abby, if she's home," Ella said, jumping on her bike. "But don't forget, it's a secret." She put her index finger to her lips and left.

Yeah, a secret. Mia smiled and reentered the house.

What she saw there made her freeze. A strange figure covered from top to toe with dark green fabric was slowly coming down the stairs. She opened her mouth, ready to scream, but then recognized the fabric. It was her curtains!

Aizek? flashed in Mia's head. *But I asked him to stay behind ... aw!*

She hurried over to the stairs and nearly ran into the strolling cat. He meowed at her angrily.

"Are you all right, Pumpkin?" She heard Mrs. Dandelion coming from the living room.

Not having a better idea for diverting her neighbor's attention, Mia yelled, "A cockroach! There's a cockroach in the kitchen!"

"Oh! Where is it?" Mrs. Rodzinski dashed past Mia with unexpected agility.

"Under the dinner table!" Mia shouted and, without losing a second, ran to the robot.

"Aizek, go back to my room, quickly!" she whispered.

The robot slowly turned around and took a leap. His foot stepped on the fabric, and the curtains slipped down. *Gosh!*

"It's escaped, the sneaky beast!" Mrs. Rodzinski reappeared in the hallway. Her eyebrows went up as she looked at the robot. "What's that?" she asked.

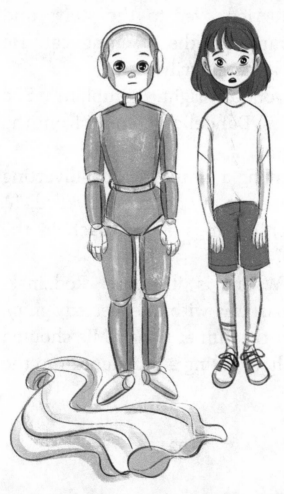

Frightened to death, Mia stared at Aizek, who stood completely still. "It's ..." she mumbled, searching for a believable explanation.

"Are your parents okay that your friends bring you such weird things?" Mrs. Rodzinski asked.

"My friends?" Mia said. "Ah, true! Ella brought me my costume ... for the end-of-year party. I'll be a robot." She forced a smile.

"Bah!" Mrs. Rodzinski made a grimace. "In my childhood, girls dressed as princesses or fairies, not hideous machines. And I'm afraid, my dear, this costume doesn't even look like a real robot."

Mia placed her hand on Aizek's shoulder, hoping he wouldn't respond.

"In my childhood, everything was better ..." Mrs. Rodzinski continued grumbling while trudging back to the living room. "Oh, the good old days ..."

Chapter 14

SHINY THINGS

"You said you would return in a minute," Aizek explained. "I waited for sixty seconds and then concluded you might be in danger and need my help. Sorry I could not come earlier. It took me time to bring the curtains down and wrap my body."

Mia smiled, folding the curtains onto her bed. She wasn't mad at him anymore. She told him about the moon rocks in the space center and how badly she wanted to see them.

"Aizek, I really can't miss that field trip." Mia left the curtains and looked at the robot seriously. "So I *have* to get that magnifying glass. But it won't be stealing," she added quickly. "We'll just *borrow* it for the science fair and then return it. Promise!"

"Promise!" Martian squawked from the bookcase top.

"Do you have a plan?" asked the robot.

"Not yet." She blushed. "Any ideas?"

"We could set up surveillance cameras around the house to see when Mrs. Rodzinski leaves the magnifying glass unattended," Aizek suggested.

Mia shook her head. "She seems to always carry it with her. And there's another little problem. We don't have any surveillance—"

Clang! Something hit the floor next to the bookcase as Martian flew by and sat on the desk. Mia picked up a shiny little object. It was an amber-stone earring. The one that her mom had lost! Or had been stolen?

"Martian, you little rascal!" Mia looked up at her pet. "Mom won't be happy to know that you took her bling," she said in her best preachy tone as he scurried around with guilty eyes.

She climbed on the chair and peeped at the bookcase top. There was a real treasury: a key, three spoons, a handful of coins, and even the glass figurine of a dolphin that Mia thought she had lost forever.

Oh no, her parrot was a serial thief! And apparently, he loved shiny things most of all.

Wait. The magnifying glass is shiny too! Mia's eyes widened. "Aizek, what if Martian can help us steal ... hmm ... *borrow* the magnifying glass?"

Someone knocked on the door. Mia's palms became clammy. Had Mrs. Rodzinski realized she had seen a real robot?

Before Mia could say anything, Aizek dodged inside the wardrobe.

He's getting better at hiding, she thought just as a smiley face popped through the doorway.

"Dad?" Mia gasped. "Why are you back so early?"

"Zach overate on marshmallows and got really sick. So much so that his parents had to drive him to hospital. But he'll be okay—don't worry, louloute," he said, smiling.

"So has Mrs. Rodzinski already left?" she asked, biting her lip.

"Yes." He looked surprised by Mia's sad face. "It seems you finally got along very well together. That's nice." Then he glanced at the materials on her desk. "How is your science project?"

"We're working on it," Mia blurted.

"We?" Her dad raised an eyebrow.

"Me and ... Martian." Mia licked her lips nervously, watching her pet grab a piece of cardboard and shred it with his beak.

Mr. Marcotte burst out laughing. "You've got a great helper!"

Martian dropped the cardboard and screeched, "Robot! Robot!"

Mia's heart sank.

"Wow, I see Martian has learned a new word. So you've read more books about robots now, eh?" Mia's dad smiled as he headed to the exit.

"I guess," she uttered, looking away.

When the door closed behind him, Mia heaved a sigh of relief.

"It is fortunate your father did not believe Martian," said Aizek, stepping from his refuge.

"I wish we didn't have to hide you," she said in a low voice. "Also, now that Mrs. Rodzinski's left, we need a new plan."

Chapter 15

THE MISSION

On Sunday morning, Mia hurried downstairs together with Martian.

Her mom smiled at her. "It's really nice, sweetie, that you offered to help Mrs. Rodzinski collect caterpillars," she said. "But please don't allow Martian to snack on them. It's not good for him."

"Sure, Mom," Mia said, blushing, and dashed outside.

When she approached the neighbor's house, she saw Mrs. Dandelion sitting in her armchair on the front terrace. She was reading a newspaper through the magnifying glass, Pumpkin lying on her lap.

Mrs. Rodzinski grinned. "Good morning, my dear! Come in! Do you want some juice or cookies or anything else?" She pointed at the small coffee table, full of treats.

Mia came closer with a shy smile. She felt Martian slightly swing on her shoulder, while his pinning eyes stared at the blinking magnifying glass in Mrs. Dandelion's hands.

"Ah, no, thanks. I've just had breakfast," Mia said, though the freshly baked cookies smelled delicious, and she wished she could try one. "May I see your tomatoes?"

"Sure." Mrs. Rodzinski guided Mia to the garden bed, where she gave her an old plastic food container and a pair of gardening gloves. "Thank you, my dear. It'll be such a great help for me."

Mia felt her cheeks burning. She breathed out when Mrs. Rodzinski finally left her and Martian alone in the backyard. Now she just needed to pretend she was looking for caterpillars and wait until her neighbor fell asleep.

It was Mia's idea to take advantage of Mrs. Rodzinski's regular morning nap with a newspaper. *But what if today is different?* Trying to chase this thought away, Mia let Martian fly freely before she put the gloves on and bent over the garden bed.

Ew! She recoiled in horror. A fat green caterpillar hung on the tomato stem. It was the most disgusting thing she had ever seen. But then she noticed another one, even bigger and uglier, under a leaf. So they weren't a product of Mrs. Dandelion's imagination after all.

Mia couldn't even think of touching any of these gross creatures. But she had to! *Well, what if I weren't in my neighbor's backyard but on Mars,* she thought, *and those little guys were a new alien species that I'd discovered?*

As she imagined that, the caterpillars immediately started looking a bit less disgusting. She slowly stretched her hand, picked one, and studied it for a few seconds. The insect had a black horn on its rear, and several white stripes and dark dots over its soft body.

What if they are intelligent? Mia continued imagining. *I should test them in my lab.* She placed the caterpillar in the food container and grabbed another one, then a few more, until she couldn't find any more.

She got so excited about her "new species discovery" that she almost forgot about her main mission. She peered round the corner of the house.

Mrs. Rodzinski was slouched in the armchair, her head resting on her chest. *Zzz!* she snored.

Cool! Mia smiled. *But where's the magnifying glass? And Martian?*

After a quick look, she noticed her pet among the branches of the apple tree that grew right next to the terrace. Her pet breathed heavily, and his yellow eyes glared.

Mia looked again at Mrs. Rodzinski. Her hands were empty, and the coffee table didn't have a trace of the magnifying glass. Strange.

Then she saw Pumpkin stretching on the terrace floor. The cat stared at Martian curiously and flipped his tail against a blinking object. Mia squinted her eyes. Yes, it was the magnifying glass! No wonder Martian wasn't happy.

Oh no! Mia rubbed her chin. There should be a way to get the cat out of their way. For example, she could tease him with something. But what did Pumpkin like? Hmm ... playing and jumping and chasing butterflies ...

Right, I'll make a butterfly! Mia pulled her pockets out and checked what she had. Her purple star-patterned sketchbook, two pencils, a few staples, and a hair elastic. That was more than enough.

She carefully tore off a sketchbook sheet without making a noise, crumpled it, and tightened its middle with the hair elastic. Would the cat take it for a butterfly? Well, she would know soon.

Removing the laces from her sneakers, Mia tied them together and attached the resulting string to the crumpled paper.

Pumpkin's eyes sparkled when he noticed the mysterious creature hopping on the terrace floor. He slowly got up and slunk toward the pray. The paper butterfly hopped a few more times and disappeared round the corner of the house. Pumpkin followed, and Mia let him catch it.

When the cat realized that the butterfly wasn't moving anymore, he lost interest and rubbed himself against Mia's legs. She bent over and petted him. He purred in response.

He's a nice cat, Mia thought. *And, well, Mrs. Dandelion is quite nice too. She even offered me her homemade cookies.*

Suddenly Mia felt that this whole mission was a bad idea. She wanted to call Martian back, but he flew by with the magnifying glass in his claws. Too late! The parrot made a circle over the back-yard and disappeared through the open window of her room.

Zzz! still came from the terrace.

Mia sighed, then tore a new sheet from her sketchbook, wrote a note, and put it under the food container.

Mrs. Rodzinski,
   I've collected all the caterpillars I could find. If you have more, please call me anytime.
          Yours,
          Mia

Chapter 16
THE FIRST DRAGONFLY

"Can we start?" Mia rubbed her hands, looking at the robot.

Aizek nodded, and the work began.

They measured and cut and taped and glued. Each time a small piece of cardboard fell onto the floor, Martian chewed it and brought it back onto the desktop, pretending to be helpful. Mia giggled. Trying to imitate her, Aizek said, "Ha-ha-ha." She burst out laughing. But after a while, his laugh became so much better that she couldn't believe it came from a robot.

When the main structure of the telescope was ready, they fixed the lenses into their places. The lens from the binoculars became the telescope's eyepiece, and the one from the magnifying glass became the objective.

Mia looked at Aizek. "Is it ready?" she whispered.

"I do not know," Aizek said. "You have to test it."

Mia carefully picked up the telescope and went to the window. She would have preferred to test it on Mars, but it was still daytime. Holding her breath, she peered through at the sparrow sitting on the fence.

"Aw, it's blurry!" she said, turning to Aizek.

"It is likely the lenses need to be focused. Slide the small tube inside the big one until you see a clear image," the robot said.

Mia followed the advice, but the sparrow still looked fuzzy. Quietly she put the telescope aside, sat on the carpet, and pulled the sketchbook out of her pocket. She tried to draw, but her eyes were blurry with tears.

Martian hopped to her and started walking around with an anxious look. "Welcome to Mars!" he sang, and bobbed his head in a funny way. Then he glanced at Mia as if checking her reaction. A weak smile appeared on her face.

"Mia, I saw water coming from your eyes. It means you are upset. What's happened?" Aizek asked.

"I told you, none of my science projects have ever worked. It was silly to imagine this one would," she mumbled, petting Martian.

After pausing for a minute, the robot asked, "How many times did you try?"

"What do you mean?" Mia lifted her head and gazed at him.

"I mean, how many times did you try to make each of your projects?"

Mia shrugged. "I guess, once."

"Then you cannot conclude that they do not work," Aizek said. "Let me show you something."

Bending down, he searched under Mia's bed and pulled out a pile of paper sheets.

"You remember you liked my drawing of a dragonfly?" the robot asked. Mia nodded. "That was not my first try." He handed the papers to her.

Mia stared at the crooked, messy lines. Probably she had drawn like this at the age of two. She passed to the next sheet. The lines became a little softer, but the doodle still didn't look like anything. She flipped through the paper sheets until she could recognize the shape of a dragonfly. Her face started brightening.

When she finally reached the beautiful drawing she had seen before, Mia jumped up.

"You're right, Aizek! I have to try again!"

Chapter 17

THE SCIENCE FAIR

When Mia arrived at school on Monday, the school canteen had been transformed into the science fair. Posters explaining scientific facts decorated the walls. The canteen tables had been converted into stands to display kids' projects.

"Class, let's start setting up before the parents arrive," said Ms. Perkins. "You can find your stands by reading the name tags."

Mia walked among the tables and quickly found her name. Right next to Zach's. Why couldn't he give her a break?

The boy was already there, laying blueberries in the shape of a pyramid near his catapult. *He must be really sick of marshmallows!* Mia thought, giggling to herself.

Zach glared at her.

Mia snorted. Her glance shifted to her backpack. What if Zach made fun of her telescope? What if everybody did? Her stomach ached with nerves.

"Mia! Come look at my cloud!" Ella called from her stand, waving.

Letting out a sigh of relief, Mia nodded and hurried over to her friend. "Where is it?" She gazed at the plastic bottle in Ella's hands. The bottle was empty with just a bit of water inside.

"You'll see in a second." Ella smiled. She squeezed the bottle with her hands and then released it. She squeezed and released a few more times. Slowly white fog filled the bottle. Mia's eyes widened.

"Doesn't it look like magic?" Ella beamed.

"Yeah. Awesome!" Mia said.

"That's not all!" Ella winked and removed the cap, letting a little donut-shaped cloud out of the bottleneck. After a few seconds, it disappeared, giving way to the next one. One after the other, little clouds appeared and disappeared until the bottle became transparent again.

"Wow, it's so cool!" Mia said, smiling.

Ella's face glowed. Then she asked, "What did *you* make, Mia? I want to see!"

The smile faded from Mia's face.

"You said it would be a surprise. I like surprises!" Ella chatted as the two girls approached Mia's empty stand. "Why aren't you set up?"

"Uh ... I was about to start." Mia shrugged. Taking a deep breath, she pulled the telescope out of her backpack. She had painted it red with tiny golden stars.

"Oh! What's that? A telescope!" Ella shouted, clapping. "You rock, Mia! I bet it's the best project!"

Zach turned toward the girls and pushed his round glasses up. "If this thing actually *works,*" he said, grinning.

Mia felt her face start to burn red. "It *does* work!" she said firmly.

"Ha! Can I try?" he asked.

As much as Mia didn't want to give her telescope to Zach, she *had* to. Or he would never believe it wasn't a fake. And it truly wasn't. After multiple tests, Mia and Aizek had found out that the telescope couldn't focus properly because the tubes were too long. Now that the tubes had been shortened, the focus was perfect.

"O-okay," Mia finally said, breathing.

Zach gave her a dazed look. Obviously, he hadn't expected her to agree.

He carefully took the instrument and aimed it at the poster explaining solar energy on the faraway wall. Soon his jaw dropped.

"Whoa! Crazy!" he yelled. "It *really* works! But why is the image upside down?" Zach turned to Mia.

"It's how it's supposed to be," she said, ready to fight back.

But the boy gave her a friendly smile. "That makes it even cooler! I'll look out the window. Okay?"

Mia nodded, blushing. *Maybe Zach isn't such a pain after all*, she thought as he jogged away.

Flop! Something green smashed against the floor.

Zach slipped, flapped his arms, and tumbled down. His glasses and the telescope flew into the air. The next second, they hit the floor next to him.

Mia and Ella hurried to the boy. "Are you okay?" they both shouted at once.

Zach winced and slowly sat up, rubbing his elbow.

Jacob came racing along. His face was white. "I'm so sorry!" He gasped. "I didn't want ... it's the slime ... it just slid out of my hands!"

"Never mind," Zach forced a grin and groped the floor around him.

"They're broken, sorry," Ella said, and passed him his glasses, which had a long crack across the left lens.

"Gosh! My parents won't be happy." Zach frowned, getting up. "Luckily, I can still see, though not as well. What about the telescope?"

"Broken too," Mia mumbled, staring at the eyepiece lens. It had shattered, along with her hopes to visit the space center. Her chin trembled.

"I'm sorry." Zach's face saddened.

"Mia, you can fix it, right?" Ella asked, looking hopefully at her friend with a weak smile.

Mia turned away, struggling to hold back her tears. She dropped the telescope on her table and started for the exit.

At the same moment, Ms. Perkins entered the canteen, followed by a tall young girl in a blue uniform. An astronaut's blue uniform!

Mia halted, blinking quickly. That girl was probably still in high school. How had she

become an astronaut so young? Mia wondered.

Suddenly her heart started racing, as she realized the simple answer. *That girl persisted!*

Mia raised her chin. She wouldn't give up either. She rushed back to the kids, sputtering, "Zach, I need your glasses. Please!"

"What for?" the boy asked with a surprised face.

"To become an astronaut!" Mia blurted out.

"What?" Zach and Ella shouted, staring at her as if she had lost her mind.

"There's no time to explain now. Just give me your glasses, please!"

"Okay," Zach said, shrugging. "But you know they're broken."

"Thanks!" Mia grabbed the glasses from his hand. "Only *one* lens is broken. I'll use the other one to replace the eyepiece in my telescope."

Chapter 18
AUNTIE!

"**Y**our telescope was a hit, louloute! I could even see Mrs. Rodzinski in her backyard from the school window," said Mia's dad, grinning, as she and her parents walked home after the science fair.

Mia giggled. She wasn't sure whether her dad was joking or whether the new lens really had made the telescope so powerful.

"Ms. Perkins did a fantastic job organizing the science fair," said Mia's mom. "And I truly enjoyed the presentation by the trainee astronaut. But I still can't believe that young girl will eventually fly to

Mars. It's such a long way!" She shook her head.

One day, I'll fly to Mars too! Mia said in her mind, smiling. But she decided it was wise to leave this announcement for another time. At least until her mom was better prepared for it.

As if listening to her thoughts, her dad asked, "Are you happy to be going on a field trip to the space center?" He winked.

"You bet!" Mia beamed. She wasn't just happy, she was *super-duper* happy! And even more so because Ella and Zach were going too.

Mia skipped down to the Marcottes' family house, impatient to tell Aizek about the broken lens and the glasses and the young astronaut trainee.

And then she saw a slim, blond-haired lady standing on the porch with a suitcase in her hand. The woman waved at her.

"Auntie!" Mia yelled, and jumped into Serena's embrace.

"We didn't know you were arriving to-day," Mrs. Marcotte said, handing Serena a cup of green tea across the table.

"*Merci!*" Serena said. "I wanted it to be a surprise. But when I arrived, there was a surprise for *me*. Nobody was home!" She laughed.

Mia sat next to her aunt, flipping through the new book that Serena had brought her. It was about the history of the greatest inventions. She smiled as she saw the telescope in there too.

After finishing her tea, Serena got up.

"Nico, Caro, let me introduce someone to you," she said with a wide grin.

Mr. and Mrs. Marcotte exchanged glances while Serena turned to the door-way.

Then the robot entered the kitchen.

"My name is Aizek. Nice to meet you all!" he said, and smiled.

Mrs. Marcotte covered her mouth with her hands.

Mr. Marcotte raised his eyebrows.

Mia held her breath. *Auntie won't let Aizek be sent back to the metal case, right?* she thought, fumbling the corner of the tablecloth anxiously.

Serena glanced at their faces and laughed. "I built Aizek for a dare. My colleagues didn't believe a robot could be as curious and smart as a real kid. And here he is!"

"Is it ... he ... safe?" Mia's mom muttered.

"Certainly! And very friendly. Even more than I expected." Serena winked, looking at her niece.

Blushing, Mia glanced at her parents, checking whether they had noticed anything, but their eyes were fixed on the robot.

"I hope you don't mind Aizek staying here," Serena said. "I couldn't leave him in Paris alone."

Please say yes! Mia thought, crossing her fingers behind her back.

"Sure," Mr. Marcotte said after a pause. "Sorry. We were just not ... prepared. You are really welcome here, Aizek."

"Thank you! It is a great pleasure for me," the robot responded, offering his hand.

Mia's dad shook it carefully, and a subtle smile appeared on his face.

"Auntie, may I show Aizek around?" Mia asked, jumping from her chair.

Before Mia's mom could object, Serena nodded, and Mia led the robot away from the kitchen.

Chapter 19

A STARRY NIGHT

"**I** guess it's dark enough," Mia whispered, standing under the oak tree and gazing at her neighbor's lit windows.

Aizek gave her a nod, careful enough not to disturb the parrot dozing on his shoulder.

"Wish me luck!" Mia said, and tiptoed to the fence. Looking around, she climbed it and leaped down into her neighbor's backyard as quietly as she could. *Luckily, Mrs. Rodzinski hates dogs*, she thought as she sneaked through the garden beds with a racing heart.

Reaching the porch, Mia pulled the magnifying glass out of her pocket and placed it in front of the back door. Then she saw a white spot glowing in the corner. She looked closer and realized it was a note held with a little stone. She picked up the note and read it.

Thank you, my dear.
I hope you made
good use of it.

Mia bit her lip and quickly made her way back to safety.

"Mission accomplished!" she whispered.

"Do you feel happy now?" the robot asked.

"Sure," Mia said, looking up at the sparkling stars in the night sky. "But there's something I'm even happier about."

"That you got selected for the field trip to the space center?"

"No." She shook her head. "That I have a friend like you!"

Aizek smiled. Then he stretched his arm toward Mia and opened his hand. There was a piece of folded paper in it.

"I drew this for you," he said, switching on the lights in his eyes so that she could see.

Mia unfolded the paper. It was a drawing of three astronauts posing next to a rocket. The astronauts were Martian, Aizek, and herself. She stared at the drawing for a minute.

"Aizek, it's awesome! And Martian looks so funny in his space suit." She giggled quietly. As if hearing that, the parrot grunted something in his sleep.

"Wait. Space suits for parrots don't exist," Mia said. "And why are *you* wear-

ing one? I thought robots didn't need ..."
She stopped, startled.

Aizek gave her his widest grin. "It must
be my imagination!"

ABOUT THE AUTHOR

Jeanne Wald was born and raised in a multicultural family, in the vast steppes of Central Asia. After obtaining a degree in International Relations, she moved to Europe, where she worked for international organizations acting in the areas of climate change, health and education. When not writing, Jeanne loves reading stories about adventurous girls, walking in the countryside and traveling. Sometimes she can be found in her partner's laboratory trying to communicate with robots, though, unfortunately, none of them is as smart as Aizek. *Mia Marcotte and the Robot* is her debut chapter book.

ABOUT THE ILLUSTRATOR

Saliha Çalişkan is a Turkish illustrator, with a degree in English Language and Literature. She specializes in children's book illustration, character design and editorial work for magazines. Her work has been published in Turkey, Canada, Ukraine and the Netherlands.

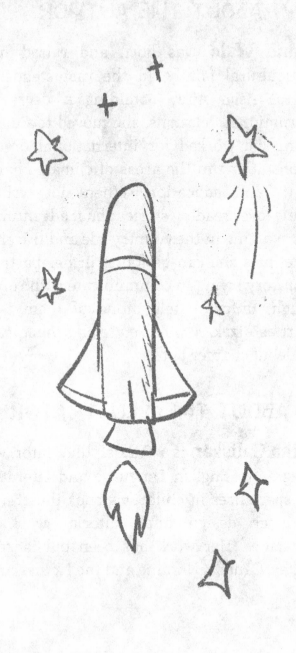

SIGN UP FOR

STEM GIRLS *Reading Club*

at www.JeanneWald.com

for exclusive content, good deals, giveaways, recommendations for STEM chapter books, and more!

Please consider leaving a review of this book. Your feedback helps other kids learn about Mia's adventures. Thank you!

9 782956 857327